GALAXY ZACK

ZACK

SCIENCE FAIR DISASTER!

By Ray O'Ryan

Illustrated by Jason Kraft

LITTLE SIMON

New York London Toronto Sydney New Delhi

LITTLE SIMON
An imprint of Simon & Schuster Children's Publishing Division
1230 Avenue of the Americas, New York, New York 10020
First Little Simon paperback edition April 2016   Copyright © 2016 by Simon & Schuster, Inc.
Also available in a Little Simon hardcover edition. All rights reserved, including the right
of reproduction in whole or in part in any form. LITTLE SIMON is a registered trademark of
Simon & Schuster, Inc., and associated colophon is a trademark of Simon & Schuster, Inc.
For information about special discounts for bulk purchases, please contact Simon & Schuster
Special Sales at 1-866-506-1949 or business@simonandschuster.com. The Simon & Schuster
Speakers Bureau can bring authors to your live event. For more information or to book an
event contact the Simon & Schuster Speakers Bureau at 1-866-248-3049 or visit our website at
www.simonspeakers.com. Designed by Nick Sciacca
Manufactured in the United States of America 0318 MTN   3 4 5 6 7 8 9 10
Library of Congress Cataloging-in-Publication Data
Names: O'Ryan, Ray. | Kraft, Jason (Jason E.) illustrator. Title: Science fair disaster!
/ by Ray O'Ryan ; illustrated by Jason Kraft. Description: First
edition. | New York : Little Simon, [2016] | Series: Galaxy Zack
; #13 | Summary: When his project malfunctions during the
Intergalactic Science Fair, will Zack, a boy from Earth
living on the planet Nebulon, be able get things
under control before disaster erupts? Identifiers:
LCCN 2015030940| ISBN 9781481458771
(hc) | ISBN 9781481458764 (pbk) | ISBN
9781481458788 (eBook) Subjects: | CYAC:
Science fiction. | Science fairs—Fiction.
| Science projects—Fiction. | Human-
alien encounters—Fiction. | BISAC:
JUVENILE FICTION / Readers / Chapter
Books. | JUVENILE FICTION / Science
Fiction. | JUVENILE FICTION /
Action & Adventure / General.
Classification: LCC PZ7.O7843
Sc 2016 | DDC [Fic]—dc23
LC record available
at http://lccn.loc.
gov/2015030940

CONTENTS

Chapter 1
Science Time

Zack Nelson stood in front of his house on the planet Nebulon. He was waiting for the Sprockets Speedybus to pick him up to go to Sprockets Academy.

Suddenly, a silver blur appeared in the distance.

There's the bus, he thought.

1

The blur stopped right in front of Zack. The bus doors opened, and he climbed on board.

The bus was filled with kids talking and laughing. As Zack headed toward the back, he overheard a bunch of conversations.

"My idea is to build a robot that can play galactic blast with you *and* transform into a hover cruiser to take you anywhere you want to go," said a boy in the front.

"I am going to build a machine that takes garbage and recycles it into

clean fuel," said a girl. "Then I am going to put that fuel into my hyper-ener-verter to power my house."

"My radioactive Surge-a-Matron will shrink atoms even smaller," said another boy as Zack walked past.

4

Zack spotted his friend Drake Taylor. Zack and Drake had been best friends ever since Zack and his family moved to Nebulon from Earth. Drake was busy scribbling on his electro-note-screen with his finger.

Zack sat down next to him.

"What's going on?" asked Zack. "When did kids at Sprockets Academy get so interested in science?"

Drake looked up. "Ever since this morning when Sprockets was picked to host the forty-second Intergalactic Science Fair!" he said excitedly.

"I remember hearing about the science fair when I first started at Sprockets," said Zack. "But I didn't realize it was such a big deal."

"It is always a big deal," explained Drake. "But it is a *really* big deal when it is held at our school!"

The intergalactic fair is held every four years. Students from all across the galaxy compete.

"Last time it was really far away, on Zog-13. This year Nebulon was picked to host. And since kids from Sprockets have always done well, we were selected to have the fair at our school!"

SPROCKET STUDENTS
DO IT AGAIN!

"Wow! That is pretty exciting," said Zack.

"Look at this," said Drake, turning his electro-note-screen toward Zack.

"I am working on a glove that has every tool built right in. But I have lots of other ideas too."

Zack turned to his twin sisters, who were sitting behind him.

"Did you two know about the fair?" he asked.

"Of course," said Charlotte. "We are already . . ."

". . . working on an experiment to see . . . ," continued Cathy.

". . . if music helps plants grow," Charlotte finished.

A few minutes later, the speedybus pulled up at the school. When Zack stepped off, he saw a 3-D holo-banner in the air. Giant letters leaped off the banner and read: PUT ON YOUR SCIENTIFIC THINKING CAPS, SPROCKETS STUDENTS! THE FORTY-SECOND INTERGALACTIC SCIENCE FAIR IS COMING!

Zack got excited. Then he immediately grew nervous. *Everyone else seems to know what his or her science project is going to be,* he thought. *I'd better come up with an idea!*

Chapter 2
The Perfect Idea

Zack hurried to his classroom and took his seat. His edu-screen blazed to life. Principal Spudnik's face filled the monitor.

"Hello, hello, my super science-minded Sprockets students!" he began.

Mr. Spudnik was usually a pretty happy guy—for a principal, anyway. But Zack had never seen him this excited.

"We are all thrilled that Sprockets Academy has been picked to host this year's Intergalactic Science Fair! I am sure that with all of your great ideas, we are destined to win the trophy again, for the fourth consecutive victory in a row! Good luck!"

Zack's teacher, Ms. Rudolph, came into the classroom. "Good morning," she began. Ms. Rudolph looked right at Zack. "For some of you, this will be your first science fair," she said. "Well, luckily we're in the same boat."

Zack felt better knowing that this competition was new for Ms. Rudolph, too. He remembered how relieved he was on his first day at Sprockets when he learned that she was also from Earth.

"I'd like you to work in groups of four, so you can help one another plan your individual projects," Ms. Rudolph said. She pressed a button on her desk-console. "I'm sending your group assignments to each of your edu-screens. Please use this time to meet with your group."

Zack's classmates' faces popped up on his screen. Underneath each face, it said: *Zack Nelson, Drake Taylor, Sally Zerbin, Rachel Vortak.*

Drake shared his ideas first. "I have so many, and I don't know where to start. One concept is a Tool-Glove that will have any gadget you'll ever need." The girls looked at him with blank faces. "Or maybe a Gravity Frisbee to use in space, or an Anti-Gravity Cup so you'll never spill your drink again!"

"Why would you want to play Frisbee in space?" asked Sally.

"And if your cup is anti-gravity, how would you drink the water inside?" said Rachel.

Sally nodded in agreement.

"I like all of your ideas, Drake," said Zack.

"I want to build a machine that can turn my drawings into 3-D movies," said Sally.

"Wow," said Zack, "that's pretty grape."

"My project is a necklace that helps you talk to animals," said Rachel. "We could finally know why dogs chase their tails, or why cats scratch furniture, or why gnorps love gwazznurffles so much."

"What about you, Zack?" asked Sally.

Zack got very nervous. He looked around the class-room. The walls were covered with pictures of some of Nebulon's natural wonders. Then Zack spotted a photo of the Topar Volcano. It was located at Nebulon's south pole.

"Maybe I'll make a volcano," Zack said. He had watched a science show on his sonic cell monitor where

someone mixed a few household items together to create a fake volcano. *How hard could it be?* he thought.

"Yippee wah-wah!" Drake, Sally, and Rachel all shouted.

"That is a great idea, Zack!" said Rachel.

Zack felt relieved. "You really like it?" he asked.

"You would definitely win if you built a volcano that spewed lava every-where," said Drake. "But where would you build it?"

"I was thinking about building it in my room, I guess," Zack said.

"Your parents will let you?" asked Drake.

"They won't mind," replied Zack.

"This I have to see!" exclaimed Drake.

"Come over after school, and I'll show you," said Zack.

Drake agreed. Zack suddenly felt confident. *Who knows? Maybe I'll win the science fair!*

Chapter 3
The Test

As soon as he got home from school, Zack hurried into the kitchen.

"Ira, I need your help," he said.

"Certainly, Master Just Zack," said Ira, the Nelsons' Indoor Robotic Assistant. "What can I help you with?"

"I need to make a volcano for a

science project," Zack explained. "Not a real one. Just something that will bubble over and look like an eruption."

"Of course," said Ira.

A few seconds later a small panel on the kitchen wall slid open. Out came a tray. It held one cup of water, one cup of vinegar, a bottle of red food coloring, and two small bowls each with baking soda and dish detergent.

"Great, Ira," said Zack. "Thanks!"

The doorbell rang just as Zack picked up the tray.

"Master Drake is here," said Ira, "and so is Seth Stevens."

"Hmm . . . I wasn't expecting Seth," said Zack. He shrugged. "Thanks, Ira."

Ira activated a code, and the front door swung open. Drake walked in, followed by their friend, Seth.

"Drake tells me you are going to make a volcano," said Seth. "No way I am missing this. It is going to be epic!"

I hope so, thought Zack.

A few minutes later, the three boys were in Zack's room.

"Protective force field, please, Ira," said Zack.

"Certainly," replied Ira.

A blue glow appeared. It covered a small square area on the floor.

"Just in case there's a mess," said Zack.

Zack placed a tall plastic container in the middle of the force field. "If this works like I hope, I'll build the mountain part of the volcano next," he explained.

Zack poured the water, vinegar, and food coloring into the container.

Seth and Drake looked at each other nervously.

Then in went the dish detergent.

Seth flinched. Drake squeezed his eyes shut tight.

"What are you guys so nervous about?" asked Zack.

"We are not nervous," Seth said quickly.

"We are . . . uh, just excited about the volcano," added Drake.

"Okay, now here goes the final ingredient to make this volcano erupt!" said Zack excitedly.

The boys jumped back, and Drake hid behind Seth.

"Wait! Stop!" cried Drake.

"What's the matter?" asked Zack.

"Please don't build a real volcano," said Seth. "We could all get hurt."

"It could destroy your entire house!" added Drake.

"It could destroy our entire city!" cried Seth.

"A real volcano?" asked Zack. "What are you talking about?" Zack poured in the baking soda. "This is just a model that imitates a real volcano."

The plastic container started to bubble. A tiny amount of sizzling goo dripped over the edge.

"That is it? That was not very exciting, Zack," said Seth disappointedly.

"No," Zack admitted. "It wasn't. This idea isn't good enough for the science fair. How will I come up with something that has a chance of winning?"

"I know!" said Drake. "We should go to the Nebulon Hall of Science. I am sure you will get grape ideas there."

Zack smiled. "Yeah! Let's go this weekend!"

Chapter 4
The Hall of Science

On Saturday morning, Zack jumped on his bike and hurried to the Nebulon Hall of Science. Drake and Seth were waiting for him out front.

"I cannot believe that you have never been here," said Seth.

"It is one of the grape-est places on

Nebulon," added Drake excitedly.

Zack looked up. The words HALL OF SCIENCE floated over the entrance to the building. The letters flashed in sparkling silver and gold lights. Above the letters a sonic cell monitor showed scenes of distant galaxies spinning in space.

"This is amazing!" exclaimed Zack.

"And that is only the entrance," said Drake.

The three friends entered the main gallery as a security camera scanned their faces.

"This museum has all the winning projects from past Intergalactic Science Fairs," said Seth. "Mine will be here soon to join the others!"

Zack and his friends stepped onto the moving walkway that carried visitors from exhibit to exhibit.

"You can climb on and off the walkway wherever you like," explained Drake.

The boys stepped off at an exhibit showing the first Nebulon space cruiser.

"There's the first sketch of the cruiser," said Zack. "It was drawn on an early version of the edu-screens we use today!"

"And there is a small scale model of the cruiser," added Drake. He pointed to a small metal model sitting on a stand.

Next to the model sat a full-size shuttle with the side opened. They were able to look at the engine compartment, the cockpit, and the passenger area.

"It looks different from today's cruiser," Zack pointed out, "but not that different."

The boys jumped back onto the moving walkway, and then they stopped at the next exhibit. This room had early versions of the Nebulon hyperphone on display.

"That first one looks like an old phone I had on Earth," said Zack. "I used to think it was the coolest phone. But then I came to Nebulon and got a hyperphone."

The second phone model had a much bigger screen. The third one had a small satellite orbiting around the phone sending signals back and forth.

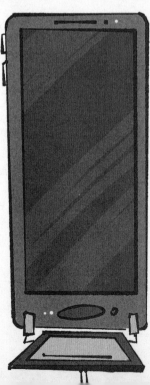

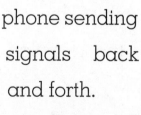

48

Zack pulled his hyperphone out of his backpack. It was smaller and thinner and had several buttons.

"Look at all the extra buttons on the earliest model," he said. "Vid-chats and everything else are now done by voice command."

The next exhibit showed the history of bikes on Nebulon. Each version was mounted on a stand. Zack noticed that the first bike looked like an old-timey version of a bike on Earth.

"Each progressive model has a sleeker look," he said. "The engines are much stronger and faster, too."

The last model was Torkus Magnus, a hyper-powered bike invented by Fred Stevens, Seth's dad. He worked at Nebulonics with Zack's dad.

"I have one of those," Seth said proudly.

As the boys continued through the hall, they saw all kinds of grape

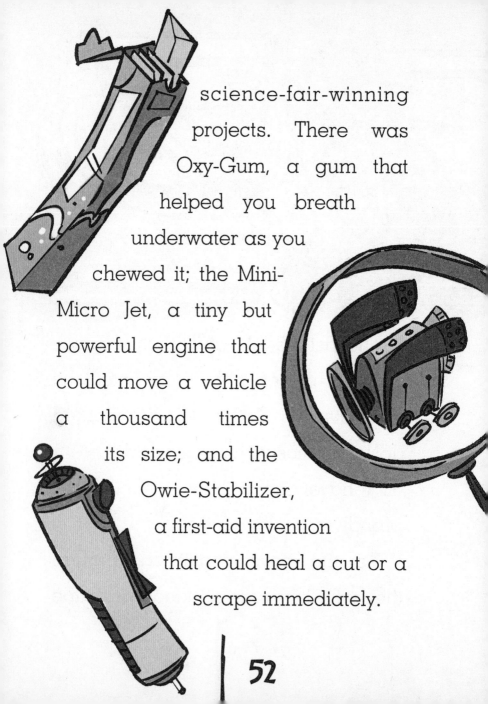

science-fair-winning projects. There was Oxy-Gum, a gum that helped you breath underwater as you chewed it; the Mini-Micro Jet, a tiny but powerful engine that could move a vehicle a thousand times its size; and the Owie-Stabilizer, a first-aid invention that could heal a cut or a scrape immediately.

"These are all fantastic!" said Zack. He felt overwhelmed, but he also started to get excited at the challenge of creating something that might win at the fair. "The only question is—what will I make?"

Chapter 5
Goo on My Shoe

The friends had been at the museum all day when an announcement blared out over the loudspeakers.

"The Hall of Science will be closing in ten minutes," said an Indoor Robotic Assistant. "Please make your way to the exit. Thank you for coming, and please visit us again soon."

"That sounds like Ira," Zack said.

"Who do you think invented Ira?" asked Seth. "A science fair winner, of course!"

Zack took one step toward the exit when he suddenly slipped. His feet shot up into the air and he landed on his back.

As soon as he hit the ground, a scientist in a long white lab coat came rushing around the corner. She had to stop short to keep from tripping over Zack.

"That is an odd place to sit down, young man," said the scientist. She looked at the floor. Then she looked left and right. She seemed very worried.

"I fell," said Zack as the scientist helped him to his feet.

"I am Dr. Zelstrum," she said. "I work here at the museum. Have you boys seen . . . um . . . anything out of the ordinary?"

"Lots of things," said Seth. "That's why Nebulites come to the Hall of Science."

"I suppose you are right, young man," said Dr. Zelstrum still looking around anxiously. Her eyes scanned the floor as she hurried away.

"Are you okay, Zack?" asked Drake.

"Yeah, I am," said Zack, looking down. "I must have slipped on something. But I don't see anything on the floor."

"Is it just me, or was that Dr. Zelstrum acting kind of weird?" asked Seth.

"It did seem like she had lost something," said Drake.

"Yeah, she lost her scientific marbles," joked Seth.

"Well, that was fun!" said Zack as the boys left the hall. "But I still don't know what I'm going to make for the science fair."

"Don't worry. You will think of something grape," said Drake.

Zack was still trying to think of a science fair project when he came home that evening.

"Did you enjoy the Hall of Science, Master Just Zack?" asked Ira as Zack came into the kitchen.

"It was grape," Zack replied. "I even learned that the first Ira was invented by a Intergalactic Science Fair winner."

"That is correct," said Ira. "The first Ira was created by Gragnix Volmed of the planet Questab in the year 2093."

Zack's dog, Luna, came bounding into the room. She jumped up and licked his face. Then she started sniffing around his shoes.

Yip! Yip! barked Luna.

"What'd you find, girl?" asked Zack.

He lifted his foot and found a big glob of green goo on the bottom of his shoe. He touched it. It felt smooth but sticky. He pressed it, and it bounced back like a sponge.

Before Zack could put his foot back down, Luna grabbed the goo between her teeth and began pulling. The gross green glob stretched like taffy.

"Come on, Luna. Let go," begged Zack.

But Luna held on tightly, tugging, and growling. The goo suddenly popped off and sent Zack and Luna flying across the kitchen in opposite directions.

Zack looked up. The pile of goo was now in the shape of his shoe. Luna slowly approached the gooey green shoe and sniffed it. The goo shoe instantly changed into the shape of Luna!

Luna dashed behind the counter. She whined and moaned as she peeked out at the fake green dog.

"Looks like I stepped in it now," said Zack. "Whatever this stuff is, maybe it can help me win the science fair!"

Chapter 6
Old Friends

The next month went by slowly for the students at Sprockets Academy. All anyone could think about was the upcoming science fair. Then finally the big day arrived.

Zack entered the Sprockets gym. The whole place was decorated with

orbiting 3-D holo-
banners, welcoming
students from around
the galaxy. Row after
row of exhibits lined
the gym.

"Hello, Zack," said
someone with a soft
voice behind him.

Zack quickly spun
around. A student with
purple fur and five
eyes towered over
him.

"Al!" he shouted.

"Great to see you again! Do you have a project in the fair?"

Zack and Al had become good friends when Al visited Sprockets and sat in on Zack's class.

"I sure do, Zack," said Al, smiling. His mouth was filled with big, sharp teeth. "I was selected to represent my home planet, Plexus."

Zack followed Al over to his display table.

A small round metal ball lifted into the air. It began orbiting around them. Then a green light flashed out of the ball onto Al's body.

"This is my De-Stinky-Fier," Al explained. "You don't need to take a shower."

"That's great!" said Zack.

"Zack!" called some-
one from across the
room. He turned
around but didn't see
anyone. All of a sudden, a
floating figure appeared
right before his eyes.

"Hector!" shouted
Zack. He had met
Hector on a visit to his
planet, Spektor. Everyone
there could float and
disappear.

"What's your project,
Hector?" Zack asked.

75

Hector held up a glowing stick. It pulsed and beeped as he moved it. "This Invisi-Wand can make anything disappear. You can even make embarrassing parents turn invisible," explained Hector, "so your friends don't have to see them."

"Boy, that could come in handy no matter what planet you're from," said Zack.

Zack spotted his sisters at the table next to Hector's.

"Listen to what . . ."

". . . we learned . . ."

". . . from our experiment, Zack," said Charlotte and Cathy.

Charlotte waved her hand over a music module. "Rockin' Round the Stars," by Zack's favorite band, Retro Rocket, blasted from the speakers.

"Isn't this a little loud for a plant?" shouted Zack.

"We learned . . ."

". . . that loud music . . ."

". . . helps plants grow!"

And sure enough, several buds on the plant blossomed into awesome-looking flowers.

"Earth to Zack!" called someone at the table next to his.

"Bert!" cried Zack, recognizing his best friend's voice. Zack rushed over to Bert's table. "You made it! What's your experiment?"

"I built a model volcano!" Bert said excitedly.

"It looks amazing!" said Zack. And it did! The rocky mountain, the glowing red lava, every detail of Bert's model looked exactly like a real volcano! Still, Zack couldn't help feeling a little bad for Bert. His own volcano idea had been nowhere close to good enough for the

Intergalactic Science Fair. But he wanted to support his friend no matter what.

Zack saw the judges starting to move from table to table.

"Okay, I have to go get ready to present my experiment," he said. "Good luck, Bert!"

"You too, Zack," said Bert as Zack raced to his own table.

81

Chapter 7
Showtime!

On the way back to his table, Zack spotted the judges standing at Drake's station. He watched as Drake demonstrated his experiment.

"How can you be in two places at once?" Drake asked the judges. "Easy. With my Holo-Double machine."

Drake flipped a switch on a small box
on the table. A second Drake appeared
beside him. "I can be here . . . ," said
Drake. Then he pressed a button on
the box. His holographic double vanished. It reappeared all the way on the
other side of the room.

"And here at the same time!" the double shouted from across the gym.

A set of twins from the planet Mirer were standing next to Drake. Everyone and everything on Mirer had a double.

"What's so cool . . . ," said one of the Mirer Twins.

"... about that? Everyone ..."

"... on our planet can do that!"

Nearby, Charlotte and Cathy also nodded in agreement.

Zack moved past Seth's table.

"I have invented a new type of gum that will help prevent cavities," Seth said to the judges proudly. "And it also blows huge bubbles."

Seth started blowing a bubble. It got bigger and bigger. Soon it was so large that it lifted Seth into the air! He floated out through an open window. His parents ran outside in a panic to catch him.

Right then, Zack heard a rumbling.
He glanced over at Bert's table and saw
that his small but real-looking volcano
was erupting. Red lava exploded from
the opening and ran down the sides of
the volcano. Everyone, including Zack,
started cheering. The judges smiled.

Zack was happy for Bert. But now
it was his turn. The judges gathered
around his table. One of the judges
was Dr. Zelstrum, the scientist from
the Hall of Science.

"I present to you—the Anything!" Zack announced. He held out his hand. The glob of green goo sat in his palm. He placed the goo next to a book. It instantly changed into the shape of the book.

He moved the goo next to his hyperphone, and it changed again. Zack moved the goo from object to object, big and small—a shoe, a bike, a galactic

sandwich, and a tiny boingoberry. Each time the goo magically took on the shape of the object.

Everyone near Zack cheered wildly. The Anything was a hit!

The judges made their marks and smiled, but Dr. Zelstrum had a puzzled look on her face. She stared at the Anything and scratched her head as she walked on to the next table.

Chapter 8
The Winner Is . . .

After the judges had seen every experiment, they huddled in private and compared their notes. A few minutes later, they had come to a decision.

"First, I want to thank the students who came from all over the galaxy to take part in the Intergalactic Science Fair," Mr. Spudnik began. "There are some amazing projects this year. Your work makes all of us very proud. Let's give a round of applause for our young scientists!"

The entire gym burst into loud applause. When the cheering died down, Mr. Spudnik continued, "And now, for the winners:

"In third place, we have Al from Plexus with his De-Stinky-Fier. In second place, we have Bert from Earth with his volcano. And in first place, we have Zack from Sprockets Academy with the Anything!"

Again, the room burst into clapping and cheering.

I can't believe I won! thought Zack. *My project will go into the Hall of Science. I'll be famous!*

The three winners walked to the front of the gym with their experiments.

"Can you all please demonstrate your experiments for everyone?" asked Mr. Spudnik.

Bert set off his volcano and red lava started overflowing from the top, while Al's De-Stinky-Fier orbited around him. Zack placed the Anything on the floor.

The small pile of green goo began to grow . . . and grow . . . and grow! Something had gone horribly wrong. The goo changed into a big green goopy monster that looked like Al with five eyes and big, sharp teeth. Then the creature began spitting out green lava all over the floor, just like Bert's volcano!

"A monster!" Mr. Spudnik shrieked. "Ruuuuuuuunnn!"

Panicked shouts filled the room as everyone ran for the doors.

Zack looked around in shock, but then it suddenly hit him. *The Anything has become the EVERYTHING, and it is now part Al and part volcano! I need a plan, and I need it fast!*

Chapter 9

Science to the Rescue!

"Drake! Al! Hector! Bert! I need your help!" shouted Zack. His friends gathered around him. "First things first. We need to get everyone out of here safely."

"I can use my experiment to confuse the monster," said Drake. He switched on his Holo-Double machine. A dupli-cate of Drake appeared on the other side of the gym, away from the exits.

"Hey, Slimy!" the Drake double shouted. "Try to catch me!"

The green slime monster reached its tentacles toward Drake's double. It

left a trail of green goo. The monster cornered the fake Drake and roared.

But when the monster reached out to grab him, Drake's double vanished. The monster crashed into the wall, covering it in slimy green goo.

While the monster was on the other side of the room, Zack led the students, teachers, and parents outside. When everyone was safe, Zack hurried back into the gym.

"I know how to stop the Everything," he said.

"Al and Bert, keep the monster distracted."

Bert and Al waved their arms.

"Hey, you!" Al shouted. "This gym is only big enough for one five-eyed huge guy. Me!"

The Everything turned and started toward Al.

With the Everything busy chasing Al
and Bert, Zack found his sisters' experiment. He grabbed the music module
and the plant, then waved his arms to
get the monster's attention.

"Hector!" Zack shouted as the monster came after him. "We need to use

your experiment! The Everything turns
into any shape it sees, so we need the
whole room to disappear!"

Hector smiled and grabbed his
Invisi-Wand. He knew exactly what
Zack had in mind. "All ready, Zack,"
he replied.

The monster slid toward Zack. It
grabbed him and the plant.

"Now, Hector!" Zack shouted.

Hector turned on his Invisi-Wand. All the kids and all the experiments in the gym turned invisible—except for the plant in the monster's tentacles. Zack lifted the music module up to the monster's face. The creature was surprised.

"Let's see what *you* think of this!"
said Zack. He waved his hand over
the music module. A nighttime lullaby
played softly in the gym. The gooey
monster transformed into a calm, little,
harmless plant.

"Yippee-wah-wah! You did it, Zack!"
Al shouted.

"You saved the Science Fair!"
added Drake.

Chapter 10
The Mimica

With the Everything under control, Hector reversed his Invisi-Wand and everything became visible again. The parents, teachers, judges, and students filed back into the gym. Dr. Zelstrum rushed toward Zack. She carried a glass case with a small force field generator attached to it.

"Young man," she said to Zack, "I thought you looked familiar when I first saw you. You were at the Hall of Science the day I lost the Mimica."

"The Mimica?" asked Zack. "What's that?"

"It is a new life form I discovered with my fellow scientists at the museum," she explained. "It can take the shape of anything. But before today it had never come into contact with any living thing outside of my lab. In this crowded room, full of living beings . . . well, let us just say that I am glad you acted quickly. Thank you for finding it."

Dr. Zelstrum slipped the glass case over the Mimica. Then she activated the force field, locking it inside. "Now I can bring the Mimica back to my lab," she said. "We have so much more we need to learn about it."

Mr. Spudnik soon stepped up to the microphone. He was surrounded by all the judges. "Zack, please come here," he announced.

Am I in trouble? Zack worried.

"We have a problem, Zack. Without an experiment, you cannot win first prize," Mr. Spudnik explained.

"I agree, Mr. Spudnik," Zack said.
"Bert should win. He won second place
with a really grape volcano!"

"That is very science *fair* of you,
Zack," said Mr. Spudnik with a wink.
"Bert, I am happy to award you first
place! Please come up and accept
your victory trophy," he announced.

Bert walked onstage. Everyone cheered wildly.

"Thank you, Mr. Spudnik and the rest of the judges," Bert said. "And thanks to Zack as well. I am honored that my volcano will be on display in the Nebulon Hall of Science. That's one more reason for me to visit Nebulon. That, and to see my best friend, Zack!"

"Now, who's up for some galactic patties, crispy fritters, and a few games of Asteroid Blast at the Starcade?" Zack asked.

Hector, Drake, Bert, and Al followed Zack out of the gym. When they got outside, Seth was still floating above the ground, dangling beneath his giant bubble. His parents were frantically jumping up and down, desperately trying to grab his feet.

"And I thought *I* had the craziest day ever!" said Zack.

All his friends burst into laughter as they walked away.

CHECK OUT THE NEXT

GALAXY ZACK

ADVENTURE!

HERE'S A SNEAK PEEK!

Zack Nelson had a huge smile on his face as he waited in line for the lunchtime Sprockets Academy space bus. It was super-hot outside, but he didn't mind. Nothing could ruin his mood today. It was the last day

Finally, when the bus arrived, all the kids climbed on board.

As Zack made his way to the back of the bus, he overheard kids talking about their summer plans.

"My family is going on vacation to Cisnos," said Seth Stevens, one of Zack's friends. "My dad got us passes to Lollyland amusement park."

"We are going to Araxie, the water planet," said Sally Zerbin, one of his classmates. "I am going to spend all summer swimming at the beach."

"I am staying on Nebulon," said another boy. "But that is okay because my parents gave me permission to go to the Starcade every day!"

Zack loved playing the games at the Starcade. Normally he would be jealous, but he had exciting summer plans of his own.

When he reached the back of the bus, Zack slipped into a seat next to Drake Taylor. Ever since Zack and his family moved to Nebulon from Earth, Drake had been his best friend.

"Are you ready for Camp Stellar, Zack?" asked Drake.

"Yeah, I can't wait!" said Zack.